OLIVIA™

Plans a Tea Party

W9-AAE-195

adapted by Natalie Shaw
based on the screenplay by Madellaine Paxson
illustrated by Patrick Spaziante

Based on the TV series *OLIVIA*™ as seen on Nickelodeon™

SIMON SPOTLIGHT
An imprint of Simon & Schuster Children's Publishing Division
New York   London   Toronto   Sydney
1230 Avenue of the Americas, New York, New York 10020

It was Olivia's favorite day of the week: Pancake Day!
"More pancakes coming right up!" said Olivia's Mom.
"Achoo!"
The pancake flew out of the skillet and landed on Ian's head with a *splat!*
Dad took over. "Why don't you take a rest?"

"I guess I do have the sniffles," said Mom. "But I have
a big party to plan, and parties don't plan themselves."
"I can help!" Olivia said. "I can be your official
assistant party planner."
Mom thought it was a great idea, and Dad said he
would take William to the park so Mom could nap.
"Olivia, I'm leaving you in charge," he said.

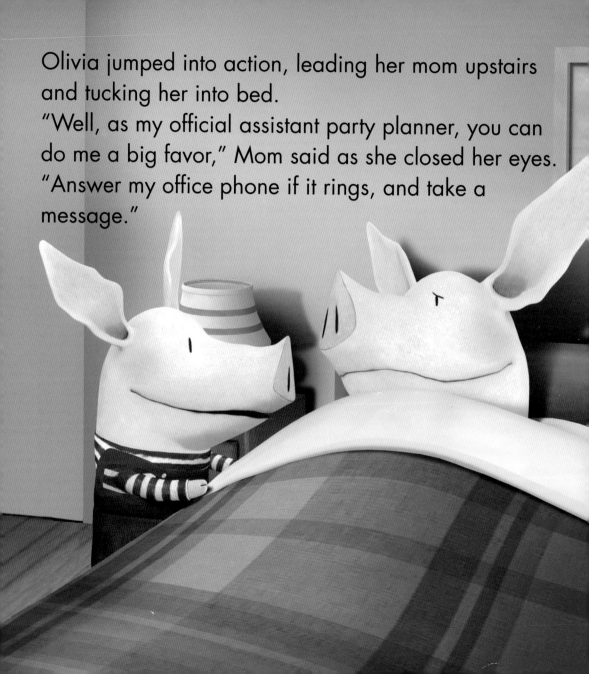

Olivia jumped into action, leading her mom upstairs and tucking her into bed.

"Well, as my official assistant party planner, you can do me a big favor," Mom said as she closed her eyes. "Answer my office phone if it rings, and take a message."

As soon as Olivia walked into Mom's office, the phone rang. She answered in her most professional voice, "Mom's Party Planning Business, this is Assistant Party Planner Olivia."

"I'm Mrs. Berkshire," said the voice in the phone. "My ladies' garden club desperately needs your help with our tea party this afternoon. Can you plan a party for me today?"

Olivia asked Mrs. Berkshire to hold and ran to Mom's room.
"Mom? There's a party emergency! The Ladies' Garden Club wants us to plan a whole tea party today!" Olivia whispered, but Mom was already fast asleep. "Mom? Mom? Okay, don't worry. I'll take care of everything."

"These sandwiches are lovely, aren't they, Winnifred?"
Mrs. Berkshire asked her friend.
But Winnifred did not agree. "Sandwiches with
chopsticks? Absurd!" she said, as Ian poured tea.
Olivia was surprised to see that no one seemed to be
having fun.
"That's because pirates don't belong at tea parties,"
explained Francine. "But Ian said that's what they wanted.
I don't understand!"

Olivia realized that the pirates weren't acting enough like pirates, so she asked them to do their very best pirate imitations.

"Hand over your treasure!" yelled Julian.

Trying to dodge the pirates, the ladies spilled their tea and knocked over chairs. The party was a lot more pirate-y. And a lot messier.

"Olivia, are you absolutely sure this is what these ladies want?" asked Dad.

"Hang on a second, Dad," yelled Olivia. "Hey, Francine! Do it!"
Francine pulled a tarp off of Olivia's wagon. She pulled a cord, and *fwoomp!* A pirate ship bounce house inflated just as Winnifred ran toward it.
"I have no treasure, I tell you," Winnifred yelled behind her, as she walked right into the bounce house.

Back at home Mom woke up from her nap and came downstairs. She'd had the funniest dream that Olivia was putting on a tea party for the Ladies' Garden Club! When she saw the mess in the kitchen, she gasped. It wasn't a dream!

"You look great, Dad! And you, too, William!" Olivia exclaimed. "All right, let's go and get this party started!" As soon as they finished setting the tables, the garden club ladies arrived. Olivia stood back and observed the party.

Olivia went to her room and opened her trunk, pulling out pirate hats, handkerchiefs, and eye patches.
"Now all we need are pirates!" said Olivia.
"Aarrgh!" said Julian.
"We have to go now or we'll be late!" Olivia said.
"Late for what?" asked Dad.
Olivia was so busy that she hadn't heard Dad and William come home from the park. That gave her an idea.

"I wonder . . . ," said Olivia.

"Arrgh, may I pour you a spot of tea, miss?" asked a pirate.

"How delightful!" said Olivia.

Olivia nodded to herself. She could definitely see it working!

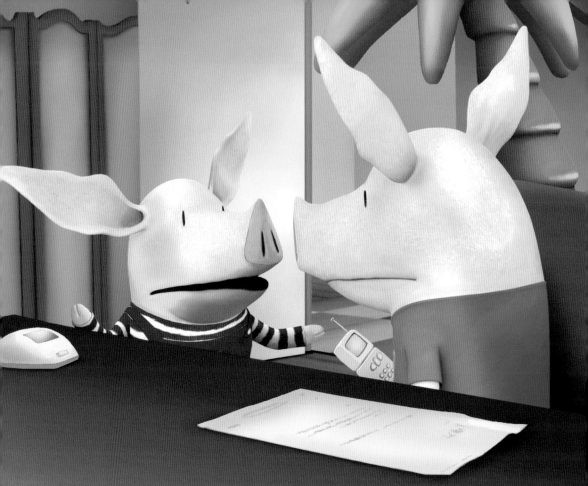

When Olivia returned, Ian told her a lady called to add
something to her party order. "Now she wants a bounce
house and pirates. Lots and lots of pirates!"
"Pirates!" Olivia asked. "Pirates at a tea party? How
would that work?"

While Olivia was away, the phone rang in Mom's office.
Ian ran to answer it, but he wasn't sure what to say.
"Hello? We, uh, plan parties?" said Ian.
"Hi, it's Oscar and Otto's mom," said a frantic voice.
"About their party . . . we still want the bounce house,
but we also want lots of pirates. Got that?"
"Yup, pirates," Ian repeated.
"Please don't come without pirates!" said Mrs. Pietrain.

cut off the crust and sliced each sandwich into triangles.
"I bet Mom would love this! I'm going to bring some to
her. Francine, you're in charge."

The food! They had almost forgotten all about it.
The trio formed a sandwich-making assembly line. Ian
spread jam, Francine spread cream cheese, and Olivia

Francine's grabbed a stack of linens from Mom's party supply shelves. "We'll need lots of these pretty napkins."
Olivia held up a pretty china plate. "And these pretty plates."
Now they had everything they would need for a tea party, and then some—except for one small detail.

When Mom arrived at the tea party, Mrs. Berkshire
approached her. "Are you the party planner?" she
asked.
Mom looked around at the pirates and bounce house
and tried to explain. "Mrs. Berkshire, I'm so sorry,"
she said. "The pirates must have been for a children's
birthday party I'm planning later this week.
Somehow they got mixed up with your tea party."

"Usually tea parties are dreadfully boring and not much fun at all," Mrs. Berkshire explained. "We rather like the pirates and bounce house . . . especially Winnifred! Look at her go!"

A delighted Winnifred ran by, yelling to Mrs. Berkshire, "You simply *must* try the bounce house! It's fabulous!"

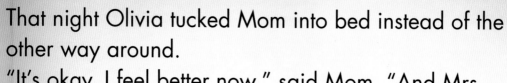

That night Olivia tucked Mom into bed instead of the other way around.

"It's okay. I feel better now," said Mom. "And Mrs. Berkshire was so happy with her tea party that she wanted you to have this."

Mom handed Olivia a red teapot.

"It's perfect!" said Olivia.

"You're perfect," said Mom, giving Olivia a big hug. "Sweet dreams!"